THE CHRISTMAS COOKIES

by Andy Rector
Illustrated by Andy Stiles

Grandma Raccoon had a bakery.
All day long she baked good
things to eat. She baked candies
and cakes and pies. Around
Christmas Grandma Raccoon
would bake Christmas cookies.
She made the best Christmas
cookies in all the town.

One day Grandma Raccoon put a sign on the window of the bakery. Everyone gathered around to read the sign on the window of the bakery. "Look," said Ernie Squirrel. "The sign says 'Help Wanted.' Let's see if we can help Grandma Raccoon."

They walked into the bakery.
They saw Grandma Raccoon
running around the kitchen. She
was out of breath.
"Grandma Raccoon," said Cara
Woodchuck, "We came to help."
"Quickly, my friends," said
Grandma Raccoon, "Put on your
aprons. I need help making
Christmas cookies."

"But first," said Grandma Raccoon, "we must move the stove closer to the table. That way we won't have to run back and forth as much."

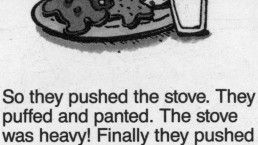

So they pushed the stove. They puffed and panted. The stove was heavy! Finally they pushed it next to the table.
"No time to waste!" said Grandma Raccoon. "It's time to make Christmas cookies!"

Soon they were all busy. Grandma Raccoon measured the flour and sugar. Ernie Squirrel cracked the eggs into the mixing bowl and poured the milk. Cara Woodchuck put sprinkles on cookies that were already baked.

"We are going to give these cookies to some special people," said Grandma Raccoon.
"Who?" asked Ernie.
Just as Grandma Raccoon was about to answer, someone walked into the bakery door.

"Hello, Darnell Deer!" said
Grandma Raccoon.
"I saw your sign," said Darnell.
"May I help?"
"Of course," said Grandma
Raccoon with a smile.
"Oh, no," whispered Cara to
Ernie. "Darnell Deer is slow and
clumsy."
"I know," Ernie whispered back.
"He will only get in our way."

Cara Woodchuck and Ernie Squirrel were right. Darnell Deer stepped on everyone's toes. He could not mix the cookie dough because his feet were too big. He bumped into the table and knocked the bag of flour all over the floor.

"I'm sorry," said Darnell. "I guess I wasn't meant to make cookies."
"Oh, that's okay," said Grandma Raccoon. "Wait. Something is wrong." She opened the stove. "The cookies are not baking, The stove is broken."
"Let me look at the stove," said Darnell. Darnell Deer looked inside the stove. He looked on top of the stove. He looked behind the stove.

"I found the problem," said Darnell. "The stove is unplugged." "We must have unplugged it when we moved the stove," said Grandma Raccoon. Everyone laughed. Grandma Raccoon plugged the stove into a closer outlet. "Now friends," she said. "Let's finish the cookies."

The next day was Christmas. Grandma Raccoon and her friends took the Christmas cookies to the special people that Grandma talked about. Who were they? They were sick children in the hospital. Darnell carried the big sack of cookies while the others passed them out to the children.

"Thanks for all your help, Darnell," said Grandma Raccoon. "You've made this a wonderful Christmas."